ANIMALS ON THE EDGE

GORILLA

ANIMALS ON THE EDGE
GORILLA

by Anna Claybourne

BLOOMSBURY

LONDON BERLIN NEW YORK SYDNEY

Published 2012 by
Bloomsbury Publishing Plc
50 Bedford Square, London, WC1B 3DP

www.bloomsbury.com

ISBN HB 978-1-4081-4825-9
ISBN PB 978-1-4081-4959-1

Picture acknowledgements:
Cover: Shutterstock
Insides: All Shutterstock except for the following; p12 © Nature Picture
Library, p13 bottom ©ZSL, p15 top ©ZSL, p15 bottom ©ZSL, p16 top ©ZSL, p18
©ZSL, p19 all images ©ZSL, p24 ©ZSL, p26 ©ZSL, p28 ©Garth Cripps/ZSL, p30
©ZSL, p31 left ©ZSL, right © ZSL, p38 ©ZSL, p39 top ©ZSL, bottom © ZSL.

Manufactured and supplied under licence from the Zoological Society of London.

Produced for Bloomsbury Publishing Plc by Geoff Ward.

A CIP catalogue for this book is available from the British Library.

Printed in China by C&C Offset Printing Co.

MIX
Paper from
responsible sources
FSC® C008047
FSC
www.fsc.org

CONTENTS

MEET THE GORILLA

With their bulging heads and big hairy bodies, gorillas can seem scary - but also very familiar. Their eyes and faces look almost human. But gorillas are wild animals, and are much stronger and heavier than us. A gorilla could easily pick up your teacher and throw them across the room! However, gorillas are mainly shy, calm and gentle, and hardly ever harm people.

Gorillas in danger

We find gorillas fascinating, yet because of human activities such as hunting, they are in trouble. In the past, gorillas lived over a wider area, and there used to be a lot more of them. Today, they are under threat. That means there aren't many left, and they could die out. If that happens, gorillas will be **extinct**, and will never exist again.

In this book you can find out all about gorillas, and why they are at risk. You can also see how people are doing **conservation** work to try to save gorillas from extinction.

Where gorillas live

Gorillas are found in thick, damp forests in Africa. Experts think there are about 200,000 gorillas in the wild. There are also about 4,000 gorillas living in zoos around the world.

This map shows where in Africa the four different types of gorilla are found.

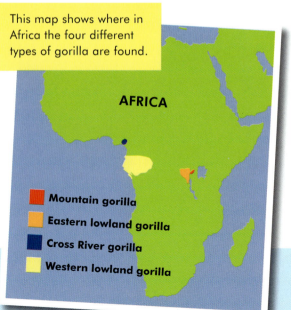

AFRICA

■ **Mountain gorilla**

■ **Eastern lowland gorilla**

■ **Cross River gorilla**

□ **Western lowland gorilla**

Four gorillas

There are two main types, or **species**, of gorilla. Each species is divided into two groups, or **subspecies**. So there are four different types altogether.

Gorilla   Human

Western gorilla
Gorilla gorilla

Western lowland gorilla
Gorilla gorilla gorilla

Cross River gorilla
Gorilla gorilla diehli

Eastern gorilla
Gorilla beringei

Mountain gorilla
Gorilla beringei beringei

Eastern lowland gorilla
Gorilla beringei graueri

The words in *italics* are the gorilla's Latin names. Scientists give each type of living thing a Latin name, so they can tell them all apart.

You are most likely to see the Western lowland gorilla, *gorilla gorilla gorilla*, in the wild and in zoos.

A Western lowland gorilla in the middle of enjoying a leafy snack.

DID YOU KNOW?

Each gorilla's nose has its own shape and pattern of lines, like a human fingerprint. Scientists can recognise a gorilla by its "noseprint"!

GORILLAS ON THE EDGE

With every year that goes by, there are fewer and fewer gorillas. They die because of hunting, diseases, and damage to their habitat – the wild forests where they live. If this doesn't change, gorillas will soon struggle to survive at all.

Staying alive

To keep going, a species has to have enough space to live in, and a certain number of animals. There must be enough to let males and females move around, find each other, and **breed** or have babies. As a species becomes rarer and rarer, this gets harder and harder. Eventually, there are not enough new babies to keep the species going, and it becomes extinct.

On the list

The **IUCN**, or International Union for Conservation of Nature, keeps a record of living things and their **status** – the situation they are in. It's called the "IUCN red list". On the list, all types of gorillas are **critically endangered**, which is the most serious status of all. It means they are close to dying out and need urgent help.

Least concern
Gray wolf

Near threatened
Greenland shark

Vulnerable
Cheetah

Endangered
Pygmy hippo

EDGE species

The western gorilla is also listed as an **EDGE** species, in the "EDGE of Extinction" programme. **ZSL**, the Zoological Society of London, run this conservation scheme to help unusual, rare animals that don't have many close relatives. EDGE stands for Evolutionarily Distinct – meaning unlike most other animals – and Globally Endangered.

Gorillas can walk upright, but more often they get around on all fours, like this.

THE STATUS OF SPECIES

The IUCN Red List can list a species as:
- Least concern – not endangered.
- Near threatened – could become endangered.
- Vulnerable – likely to become endangered.
- Endangered – at risk of dying out.
- Critically endangered – at very high risk of dying out.
- Extinct in the wild – Only survives in zoos or protected areas.
- Extinct – Gone for good.

GORILLA IN THE MIRROR

Humans and gorillas belong to the same animal family – the apes. Gorillas can stand up and walk, make faces, and use objects as tools, like we do. Like us, they are clever and good at learning. They are among our closest animal cousins.

Critically endangered
Western lowland gorilla

Extinct in the wild
Kihansi spray toad

Extinct
Great auk

GORILLAS AT HOME

In the wild, gorillas are the ultimate jungle creatures. They live in hot, damp rainforests, mountain forests, bamboo forests, and squelchy jungle swamps.

Wet and warm

Where gorillas live, the weather is warm, but often wet. In some forests, it rains every day; in others, there's a rainy season for part of the year. This **climate** makes it easy for lots and lots of plants to grow, giving gorillas their food.

A gorilla troop eating and lazing around together in the undergrowth.

Gorilla groups

Most gorillas live in family groups called **troops**. A troop can have up to 20 gorillas in it. There are usually several females, their babies and older children, and one old male, who leads the troop. He is called a **silverback**, because once they are old enough – around 12 years old – males start to grow silvery hair on their backs.

The females in a gorilla troop often have small babies, and carry them around.

SPEAK GORILLA!

Rrrooarr! The silverback makes this call to warn of danger.

Hoo-hoo-hoo The silverback has spotted another gorilla troop.

Grunt grunt! Short grunts mean "get out of my way" or "give me that!"

Aaargh! A loud scream means a gorilla is upset or fighting.

Prrrr... hmmm... Soft purring, mumbling sounds mean "I'm happy".

In this photo you can see some of the silver hair at the top of this old male gorilla's back.

A nest for the night

A troop of gorillas has its own home area, or **range**, but no fixed home or den. Instead, the gorillas wander around their range, looking for food. Every night, when they want to sleep, they build a brand-new nest out of leaves and branches. Western lowland gorillas sometimes build theirs in a tree, as they are good at climbing.

Can gorillas talk?

As the gorillas in a troop **forage** and explore, they make howling, grunting or hooting noises to tell each other where they are, and to send messages. Scientists have found that they have more than 20 different calls, all with different meanings.

ARE GORILLAS DANGEROUS?

A gorilla is easily strong enough to kill a human, but they are mainly quiet and peaceful animals. However, a silverback will always defend his troop from danger. If a human, or other animal, threatens the troop, he might chase and bite them.

FAMOUS GORILLA ENCOUNTERS

Despite being so rare and shy, gorillas are very well-known, popular animals. This is partly thanks to some very famous gorillas, and some famous humans who have introduced us to them.

Gorillas on TV

In 1979, TV viewers in Britain were thrilled to see the well-known wildlife presenter David Attenborough snuggling up to a troop of mountain gorillas, in his popular programme *Life on Earth*. He didn't plan to get so close to them, but they were very friendly and welcoming, and soon surrounded him. One baby even lay on top of him!

Not so scary

Traditionally, people thought of gorillas as fierce and scary – probably because they are so big and strong. Old films such as *King Kong* often made them seem like terrifying monsters. But Attenborough's gorilla encounter changed many people's minds about gorillas – it showed that they were gentle and peaceful.

A young gorilla uses David Attenborough as a cushion in the famous *Life on Earth* footage.

Dian Fossey

The gorillas Attenborough met lived in Rwanda in Africa, and were already familiar with humans. An American gorilla scientist, Dian Fossey, lived there for many years, studying the gorillas and trying to stop people from hunting them.

Fossey taught the world a lot about gorillas by writing books and articles about them. Sadly, she was murdered in Rwanda in 1985. Her bestselling book *Gorillas in the Mist* was made into a film about her.

Dian Fossey's gravestone in Virunga National Park in Africa, marked with the words "No one loved gorillas more".

GUY THE GORILLA

Guy was one of the most famous animals ever to live at ZSL London Zoo. He arrived there as a baby in 1947, and lived to the age of 30. He became the zoo's most popular attraction. He was huge – almost as tall as a man, and three times as heavy. When he stretched out his arms they measured 2.7m across. But he was very gentle too. Members of the public loved him so much, they would send him birthday cards, and presents of fresh fruit.

LEARNING LANGUAGE

Koko, a female gorilla kept at San Francisco Zoo in the USA, is famous for learning to "talk" to humans using sign language. The scientist who taught her, Dr Penny Patterson, says she can make about 1,000 different signs, and understand 2,000 words.

Guy the gorilla in a photo taken around 1970. He looks grumpy here, but was gentle and friendly.

GORILLAS IN THE ZOO

Most of the gorillas that live in zoos are western lowland gorillas. Today, as they are endangered, keeping them in zoos helps their species to survive.

Living together

In the wild, gorillas live together in groups. They are happiest if they can do this in the zoo, too. A zoo **enclosure** for gorillas must have enough space for several gorillas to wander around, explore, exercise, and behave as naturally as possible.

A place to nest

Western lowland gorillas can walk on the ground, but they also love to climb. So their enclosure should have trees to climb and nest in, or something to use instead of a tree. Some zoos have climbing frames for their gorillas, with special nesting places in them. They give the gorillas piles of branches or hay, so that they can build their own nests, just as they like them.

Western lowland gorillas at a zoo explore their log and rope climbing frame.

DID YOU KNOW?

Sometimes, the male gorilla likes making his nests on the ground, while the females make theirs somewhere high up.

Gorilla science

Gorillas live in zoos partly to help their species survive. Scientists work with zoo gorillas to test out ideas they can then use in the wild. For example, ZSL scientists came up with a way to find things out about a gorilla – such as whether it's male or female – by looking at its poo. This is now used to help keep track of wild gorillas.

A zookeeper hands a gorilla a tasty treat, a fresh banana.

Gorillas seem to enjoy playing with bouncy balls, just like us.

FUN THINGS TO DO

Just like humans, gorillas like playing with toys. Zookeepers give them fun things to play with, like balls, rope swings, tyres, and woolly material to touch and add to their nests. Gorillas also enjoy searching for their food, instead of just having it handed to them. So keepers scatter food around the enclosure, sprinkle it among the grass, or hide it in unexpected places.

FEEDING TIME

Gorillas have big, sharp teeth and can look fierce - but they are almost completely vegetarian. The only animals they eat are ants, caterpillars and other creepy-crawlies, which get swallowed along with mouthfuls of leaves and fruit.

In the wild

Wild gorillas spend about half of each day wandering around, finding and eating plants. They feed for a few hours in the morning, have a rest, then eat some more. They like lots of different plant parts – leaves, stems, bark, roots, twigs, **shoots**, fruits, nuts and even flowers.

Western lowland gorillas eat more fruit than other gorillas – it's the biggest part of their diet. They're good at climbing trees to get to the tastiest fruit.

FRUIT ICE LOLLIES

In very hot weather, some zookeepers help gorillas cool down by giving them frozen fruits, such as watermelon, or iced tea.

Western lowland gorillas like to find a comfortable perch in a tree.

ZOO GORILLA FOOD SHOPPING LIST

lettuce
popcorn
swedes
cucumber
browse (tree branches)
sunflower seeds
fruit tea
vitamin pellets
pak choi
carrots
pecan nuts
broccoli
sweet potato
pak choi
apples, oranges and bananas for treats!

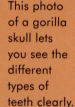

A mother gorilla holds her baby tightly while munching on an orange.

In the zoo

Zoo gorillas eat about 5kg of food each a day – equal to about 50 bananas! But to make things more interesting, zookeepers give them lots of different fruits, vegetables and plants. Gorillas don't usually drink much, as their food, such as cucumbers, contains a lot of water.

In the past, some zoos used to feed gorillas on cereals and sugary foods to make sure they got enough energy. But some gorillas got diseases such as **diabetes** and heart disease, caused by an unhealthy diet. So zoos have now switched to a fresh plant diet.

Gorilla teeth

Gorilla teeth are a bit like ours. They have front teeth, or incisors, for biting, and molars for chewing. Adult males also have long, sharp canine teeth, like a wolf's or a tiger's. But they aren't for eating meat. Instead, the males use them to attack enemies, or sometimes to fight each other.

This photo of a gorilla skull lets you see the different types of teeth clearly.

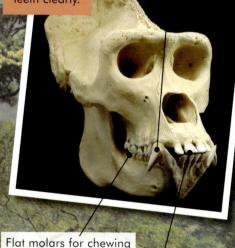

Long, sharp canine teeth for biting and fighting

Flat molars for chewing

Sharp incisors (or cutting teeth) for biting

A DAY IN THE LIFE: GORILLA KEEPER

Maddie Gordon works at ZSL London Zoo as a Senior Keeper, looking after the western lowland gorillas. She explains all the jobs a gorilla keeper has to do, and what gorillas are like when you get to know them...

A day with the gorillas

8.30am Carrying a large bucket of vegetables, it's time to go and say good morning to Kesho the male western lowland gorilla, and the three females – Zaire, Effie and Mjukuu.

9.00am Once they're tucking into their breakfast, it's time to clean their living room, which we call "The Gym". We have to pick up all the uneaten food from yesterday, and all the poo they so kindly leave for us!

10.00am We go outside to the gorillas' outdoor area, and throw the rest of their breakfast around all over the grass – searching for it keeps them busy! After a bottle of fruit tea each, the gorillas come out to finish their breakfast.

Maddie Gordon at work at the gorilla enclosure, in her London Zoo uniform.

THE GORILLA TEAM

There are seven of us who work with the gorillas. We know them well, and they know us well. It's best if the gorillas have a good relationship with you. It's one reason not many people work with them – they have to get to know you and trust you.

Maddie with Effie, the hungriest of the four gorillas she helps to look after.

12 noon The gorillas have some peanuts, pecans, seeds or unsweetened popcorn as a snack before lunch. Effie loves it! Her favourite thing in the world is to eat, eat and then eat some more.

1.30pm Lunchtime for the gorillas, including some more vegetables, and some browse or tree branches. They love willow branches best. We offer them another drink too.

4pm Towards the end of the day, after a nice snooze, the gorillas go charging into their night-time dens and await their dinner. Zaire will sit and look at you and snap her fingers as if to say, "Waiter! Any time before Christmas preferably!"

5pm After dinner, we say goodnight to the gorillas. They'll make a happy grumbling sound in reply – except Effie, who's still too busy munching!

London Zoo's western lowland gorillas, from top to bottom: Mjukuu, Kesho, Effie and Zaire.

GORILLA BABIES

Gorillas are closely related to humans – and that could be one reason why, when we see a baby gorilla, we think it looks so cute! For gorillas, though, having babies isn't always easy.

Gorilla families

In the wild, a leading silverback gorilla mates with the females in his troop, so he is the father of all the troop's babies. When a baby is born, it's quite small, about half the size of a human baby. Its skin is pale and pinkish, and it has hardly any hair on its body.

Look after me!

Like a human baby, a baby gorilla is helpless and needs its mother to look after it. It will cry and wail when it's hungry or wants a cuddle. Gorillas are **mammals**, which means the mother makes milk in her body to feed to the baby. She carries her baby around with her constantly, and shares a nest with it at night.

A baby gorilla feels safest snuggled up close to her mum.

In the zoo

To help zoo gorillas mate, keepers match males to females, and hope that they will breed and a baby will be born.

Not many babies

Western lowland gorillas have a long **gestation** period – the time it takes for a baby to grow inside its mother before being born. It also takes several years for the baby to grow up and start looking after itself. A mother gorilla only has one baby at a time, once every 4-6 years. And sadly, it's quite common for babies to die soon after birth. All this means that if gorilla numbers fall, because of poaching or disease, it's very hard for them to bounce back quickly.

Male and female gorillas nuzzling each other as they get ready to mate.

Babies cling tightly to their mother's fur, so they can go everywhere with her.

FACT FILE: STAGES

These are the stages a gorilla goes through as it grows up:

Gestation: 9 months

Birth weight: about 2kg

Birth to 6 months: Clings to its mum and feeds on her milk.

6-8 months: Starts eating plant food as well as milk.

7-9 months: Starts learning to walk and climb.

2-3 years: Stops feeding on milk.

7-9 years (females) 12-14 years (males): Adult and ready to breed.

Gorilla lifespan: up to 50 years in captivity.

ONE GORILLA'S STORY: ZAIRE

This is the story of Zaire, a western lowland gorilla who has spent her whole life in captivity.

Born on an island

On 23rd October 1974, a new baby gorilla – a girl – was born at Jersey Zoo, on the island of Jersey in the English Channel. Her father was the silverback Jambo, and her mother was called Nandi.

Unfortunately, Nandi wasn't looking after her new daughter, so the keepers had to raise her themselves. Because her first few years were spent in the company of humans, Zaire – as the baby was named – was very comfortable around people.

On the move

Zaire lived at Jersey until, in 1984, aged nine, she was moved to ZSL London Zoo. There she met her mate, a large silverback named Kumba. She lived in an enclosure with Kumba and another female, Salome. Zaire soon became Kumba's favourite.

Zaire in a typically stubborn, uncooperative mood.

CARING JAMBO

Zaire's father, Jambo, became world-famous in 1986, when a five-year-old boy, Levan Merritt, fell into the gorilla enclosure at Jersey Zoo. Jambo crouched over Levan, stroked him, and kept the other gorillas away, until he could be rescued.

Becoming a mum

By 1985, Zaire was expecting a baby of her own. This pregnancy wasn't successful – but Zaire did finally have a baby girl two years later, on 1st July 1987. Keepers at London gave her a **Swahili** name, Kamili, meaning "Perfect". Zaire turned out to be a great mum. Kamili stayed with her until 1993, when she was moved to Belfast Zoo to start her own family. Kumba and Salome also moved away a year later.

New friends

Since then, Zaire has remained a constant and much-loved member of ZSL London Zoo's gorilla troop – and new gorillas have come to join her. She now lives at the zoo's Gorilla Kingdom, with two other females, Effie and Mjukuu, and their silverback, Kesho. In Belfast, her daughter Kamili became a mother too – so Zaire is now a grandma!

Zaire enjoys some exercise on the gorillas' tree and rope climbing frame.

KNOWING ZAIRE

Zaire's keepers say she has a stubborn, but funny personality. When they call her, she often refuses to answer. When they want her to move somewhere, she'll go the other way! But she's a gentle, calm gorilla who is kind to the others in her troop.

Zaire sits calmly with one of her companions while feeding.

THREATS TO GORILLAS

The population (number) of western lowland gorillas has fallen fast. There are more than we once thought, as around 125,000 gorillas were discovered in Congo in 2008. But they still face several serious threats, which are getting worse.

Habitat loss

To survive properly, gorillas need their natural habitat – thick, wild forests, with lots of different plants and trees. But humans often destroy forests by **logging** – cutting down the trees for timber (wood), and to make space for farms and towns. When habitat is destroyed, it's called **habitat loss**. Today, logging in Central Africa is increasing, making it a bigger and bigger threat for the gorillas.

Loggers use big machines and trucks to cut down and move trees quickly, meaning they can cause a lot of damage to forests.

Hunting

It might be hard to imagine eating a gorilla, but it does happen. **Poachers** (illegal hunters) kill them for their meat, along with other wild species like monkeys, hippos and even elephants. Wild animal meat is called **bushmeat**. Some people catch and eat it themselves, but it's also taken to towns and villages to be sold in markets.

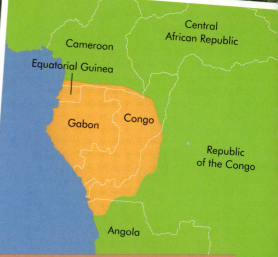

Hunting gorillas is against the law in Central African countries, but it's very hard to stop people from doing it. They may desperately need the meat for food, or to make money to survive.

Deadly disease

Since the 1970s, a deadly new disease called Ebola has been spreading across parts of Africa. It's now one of the worst threats facing gorillas. Scientists have found that if the Ebola **virus** (germ) infects a group of gorillas, only 5%, or one in every 20 gorillas, will survive.

HELPING THE HUNTERS

Bushmeat hunting and logging are closely linked. Logging clears roads and spaces in the forest. This can allow poachers to reach areas that were once too remote to hunt in.

WHAT IS EBOLA?

Ebola is a horrible disease that makes body parts such as organs and blood vessels stop working properly. It is deadly, and is thought to have killed many thousands of wild gorillas. Humans can catch it too, sometimes from infected bushmeat.

War

Gorillas are also affected by **civil wars**, where different armies fight for control of a country. In a war, law breaks down and it becomes easier to hunt and kill gorillas and sell their meat. It's also harder for conservation workers to reach gorilla areas.

Central African Republic

Cameroon

Equatorial Guinea

Gabon

Congo

Republic of the Congo

Angola

Western lowland Gorillas live in the countries of Gabon, Republic of the Congo, Central African Republic, Equatorial Guinea, Angola and Cameroon. Of these, only Gabon has avoided civil war or unrest in the past 50 years.

HELPING GORILLAS

Gorillas are in a very serious situation. For lots of different reasons, they are dying faster then they can breed and make up their numbers. So how can we help them?

ZSL at work

The Zoological Society of London (ZSL) runs conservation schemes to help many endangered animals, including gorillas. It combines studying gorillas in the zoo, with sending people to work in wild gorilla habitat in Africa.

ZSL conservation worker Chris Ransom with his team, studying gorilla tracks and signs in the forest.

Understanding the gorilla

One of the most important jobs is to study and **monitor** (keep track of) wild gorillas. We really don't know how many western lowland gorillas there are, and where exactly they live. Conservation workers have to go deep into the forest to count gorilla poos and nests, to work out how many gorillas live in each area.

Schoolchildren in West Africa now learn about protecting rare wild animals, such as gorillas.

MAKING CHANGES

For many people, it's traditional and normal to hunt wild animals. The problem is that there are now so many people, hunting could wipe out rare wild species like gorillas. Some conservation programmes teach schoolchildren and local people about endangered species, and how to protect them.

EBOLA ACTION

As Ebola is such a big problem for gorillas, scientists are studying that too. They are working on a **vaccine** that could prevent the disease, and finding out the best ways to give it to wild gorillas.

Safe places to live

In the countries where gorillas live, there are several **national parks** and **wildlife reserves**. These are wild areas that are supposed to be protected from logging, poachers, or anyone farming or building there. But in poor or war-torn countries, there may not be enough money to protect the parks properly. Conservation schemes can help with this by raising money and sending experts to help run parks.

New parks

Opening new national parks will also help gorillas. Once scientists find out where gorillas are doing well, they can work with Central Africa governments to decide on good places to put new protected areas.

FINDING OUT THE FACTS

The jungles where gorillas live are thick, hot and damp. It's easy to get lost, and some of the wildlife there, such as snakes, can be dangerous. All of this makes it easier for gorillas to hide – and harder for scientists to study them!

Gorilla tracking

It's incredibly exciting to see gorillas in the wild – but that's not always how gorilla monitoring works. To find out where they live, and how many of them there are, scientists mainly rely on **tracking** methods. They look out for signs of gorillas – such as their nests, droppings, and damage to plants they have been eating. They also listen for sounds the gorillas make, like munching and chest-beating.

When a western lowland gorilla is up a tree, it can be very hard to spot from the ground.

A fresh gorilla poo like this one is a sign that gorillas have been in the area recently.

SPOT THE GORILLA SIGNS!

- Gorilla nest
- Broken food plants
- Gorilla footprints
- Gorilla knuckleprints
- Gorilla poo
- Gorilla diarrhoea
  (Yuk! Ebola and some other diseases can give gorillas diarrhoea, so this can be a sign that the local gorillas aren't very healthy.)

Watching the poachers

Besides tracking gorillas, conservation workers also look for signs of poaching, and watch out for poachers. This can be a bit nerve-racking, as poachers aren't always very friendly, and some have guns.

Working together

Scientists and conservation workers from outside countries often work with local people to track gorillas. Park rangers, who work in national parks, know where to find wildlife and are good at spotting the signs. They may also know how poachers operate and who they are.

Sometimes, a conservation programme trains local people and pays them to do work such as tracking and monitoring gorillas. As this makes them a living, it can help them become more interested in saving endangered species and stopping poaching.

The tool shown here is a machete – a large, sharp knife that's useful for cutting your way through the forest.

Gaboon vipers live in the same areas as gorillas. They have very long fangs and deadly venom.

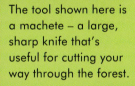

AHEM!

If you're tracking gorillas and suddenly find yourself close to a gorilla troop, making a low, grunting "Ahem!" noise can help to keep them calm. In gorilla-speak, it means "I won't hurt you".

A DAY IN THE LIFE: GORILLA TRACKER

Chris Ransom is a conservationist working for ZSL on projects in Africa. He describes what it's like to spend a day in the forest, monitoring western lowland gorillas.

Chris in his trusty baseball cap, which protects against both sun and rain in the tropical jungle.

Base camp

An expedition into the forest to monitor the gorillas takes three weeks, so we need somewhere to stay. We set up a base camp from which we can easily explore the areas where gorillas might be living.

The day begins

We awake in the dark at three or four in the morning, and light a fire to heat up our breakfast. There are no luxuries in the field – breakfast is normally reheated rice and beans from yesterday's dinner. After breakfast, we get our kit together and set off into the forest.

CHRIS'S KIT FOR A DAY IN THE FOREST INCLUDES:

A water bottle (we collect water from the streams during the day)

Iodine to kill germs in the water, and orange powder to make it taste nicer!

GPS

Binoculars

Log book

Snacks and something for lunch, such as tinned sardines and biscuits.

Wellies (walking boots don't last five minutes in the soggy jungle)

Tough, lightweight trousers

T-shirt and baseball cap!

On the trail

To follow the gorillas, we need help from local trackers, who are experts at spotting gorilla signs such as knuckle prints, or plants that have been disturbed. Once they find the gorillas' trail, we begin to follow it. We look out for more clues, like half-eaten fruit, and gorilla poo. We note everything down in our log books, and take samples of poo for testing. The tests can reveal things like what the gorillas have been eating, or what diseases they carry.

We usually stumble across a gorilla nest site. The empty nests can tell us a lot about gorillas, like how high they like to nest, and which trees they prefer. We also collect hairs from the nests for testing.

Heading home

Time flies as we excitedly note down our discoveries, and it's soon time to head back to base camp. Negotiating the forest after dark is very difficult, so we always aim to be back at camp by 5pm. Everyone is exhausted, so we're all tucked up in our tents by 8pm, dreaming of the next day's adventures.

Collecting and sorting out gorilla poos is one of the smellier parts of the job!

POACHER ENCOUNTER

We come across poachers once in a while, but they know what they're doing is illegal, so they normally flee when they spot us. However, we were once removing snares set by poachers when we heard that they were coming after us. Poachers can be dangerous and often carry guns, so we made a quick exit!

Getting around in the jungle can involve some hairy moments, like this one!

NATIONAL PARKS

For an endangered gorilla, a national park is one of the safest places to be in the wild. As long as they have enough money and are properly run, national parks let wildlife live naturally, while protecting it from danger.

What is a national park?

A national park isn't like a little local park. It's a big, sometimes huge, area of land, kept in a wild, natural state (or as near to it as possible). The government of a country owns and controls its national parks. Hunting wildlife and damaging habitat are banned, but people can visit to watch wildlife.

As a way to help gorillas and other wildlife, ZSL works with two important national parks in Africa: Virunga and Lopé.

AFRICA

Gabon

Virunga National Park

Lopé National Park

Rwanda

Democratic Republic of Congo

This map of Africa shows the locations of Virunga and Lopé National Parks.

DID YOU KNOW?

The first national park in the world was Yellowstone, in the USA, founded in 1872. Today, most countries around the world have national parks.

Virunga national park

Virunga is Africa's oldest national park. It covers an amazing mixture of rainforests, lakes, swamps, grasslands and volcanoes. But the Democratic Republic of Congo, where it lies, has had a lot of wars, and Virunga has been attacked, ransacked and fought over. Now, things are improving. ZSL has helped to pay for new buildings and fences, as well as tracking wildlife and training people to be **park rangers**.

Lopé National Park

Lopé National Park is in Gabon, one of Africa's wealthier and wilder countries. 80% of Gabon is still covered in forest, and it has lots of national parks. Lopé is one of the biggest. It's home to all kinds of interesting species, like forest elephants, forest buffaloes, leopards, and the rare sun-tailed guenon monkey.

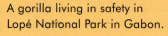

A gorilla living in safety in Lopé National Park in Gabon.

This park ranger in Virunga National Park in Rwanda carries a gun for protection.

BEING A PARK RANGER

Park rangers work in national parks. They patrol or "range" around the park to check on the wildlife and look out for damage, poachers or animal traps. In some parks, they even chase and catch poachers. They also give advice to visitors, repair damaged bridges and pathways, and sometimes help scientists by tracking and monitoring wildlife.

MAKING CHANGES

To help gorillas, it's important to change the way we do things, to make life easier for them. Local people don't have to hunt gorillas if they have other, better jobs. If they know that bushmeat can give you Ebola, they might prefer to avoid it. And big companies can do mining and logging in new ways, that affect wildlife less.

The problem with poaching

Hunting wild animals to eat was not always a problem. In the past, when there weren't so many people, and the forests were enormous, it made sense. People took a few wild deer, monkeys or other animals, but these species still survived.

Today, in many parts of the world, things are different. When animal species are endangered, and their wild habitats are disappearing, hunting can wipe a species out. Once it is extinct, it's gone forever —and so is the hunters' way of finding food or making a living.

Visiting wild areas to watch wildlife and take photos is better than hunting rare species.

Gorillas can be hard to spot in the wild, and local people are often the best at knowing how to find them.

Conservation jobs

Working in conservation can change all this. It makes money from endangered species without them having to die. In some areas where gorillas live, conservation workers train local people to work as park rangers, forest guides and trackers.

It works!

This is one of the most successful types of conservation invented so far. Besides helping people make a living, it also means they want the forest and its animals to survive, so that they can keep their jobs. The same method is being used all around the world, to help many other kinds of endangered species.

GORILLAS AND GERMS

One way for scientists to understand gorillas better is by studying gorilla poo. They collect the poo and look at it closely through microscopes to check for germs. They are learning more about how diseases spread from gorilla to gorilla, and from human to gorilla. With this information, they can show local people how to avoid catching germs from gorillas, or giving germs to them.

Gorillas don't just need to survive – they also need the forests to survive, to provide them with food and a home.

BELINGA-DJOUA

In an area of Gabon called Belinga-Djoua, scientists are studying how the Ebola virus and mining in the forest have affected western lowland gorillas. This information could help mining companies change the way they work, and find ways to stop gorillas dying from disease.

CONSERVATION BREEDING

If you go to a zoo to see the gorillas, you might be lucky enough to see a baby too! When zoos help animals to breed and have babies, it's called conservation breeding.

Staying alive

Conservation breeding can help endangered species, as long as they breed well in **captivity**. It keeps a population of animals alive, safe and healthy, even when they are at risk in the wild. As in the wild, gorillas in zoos don't have babies all that often. But a lot of zoos have breeding programmes, especially for western lowland gorillas – and there have been plenty of successful births.

GOING WILD

If conservation breeding goes well, zoos sometimes release endangered species from the zoo into the wild. This is called **re-introduction**. It can help endangered species survive in the wild - as long as there's a safe place to re-introduce them to. Some conservation groups have begun re-introducing gorillas to protected areas in Gabon.

A baby gorilla cuddles close to his mum.

Who's who?

Conservation breeding takes a lot of planning! Zoos around the world exchange gorillas with each other, so that males and females can be matched up to mate. They also keep records called **studbooks**, showing all the babies that have been born and who their parents were.

CUTE BABIES!

When a zoo gorilla has a baby, it can be a big bonus for the zoo. The birth is usually reported in newspapers and on TV, and visitors flock to the zoo to see the baby. This raises extra money for zoo care, more conservation breeding, and conservation in the wild.

Helping hand

Sometimes, zoos can use medicine to help gorillas get pregnant. Salome, a western lowland gorilla at Bristol Zoo England Gardens, was trying to breed, but was not having any babies. The zoo decided to give her a medicine that's also used to help humans have babies. It worked, and Salome had her baby boy Komale in 2006 – followed by a new baby in 2011.

A baby zoo gorilla peeps out from behind her mum to look at her visitors!

ONE GORILLA'S STORY: BABY RESCUE

Poachers often kill an adult gorilla for its meat, and then discover it has a baby with it. Baby gorillas are too small to make a worthwhile meal, so instead they are captured alive, and sold at a market or kept as pets – that is, until they become too big.

Escape from the market

ZSL conservationists found one baby gorilla that this had happened to, for sale at a local market in north eastern Gabon. Although it is illegal to sell gorillas, very poor people often feel like there's no alternative – it's their only way of making a living.

Story of the rescue

When we discovered the baby western lowland gorilla, we began negotiations with the person who was selling it. We will never exchange money for an animal, as this just encourages more and more illegal trade in endangered animals. Instead, we managed to convince the man to hand over the baby gorilla for free. If he had refused, we could have called in the local authorities to help us.

A baby gorilla is much smaller than an adult and is not much use as bushmeat.

NO NAME

Conservation and sanctuary workers sometimes give names to the gorillas they work with – but this gorilla didn't have one. What would you call him?

Besides tracking and caring for wildlife, ZSL workers talk to local people, to try to help them live alongside gorillas without harming them. They explain wildlife laws, and inform them about the health risks of bushmeat, which can actually make you very sick.

Wildlife sanctuary workers can feed baby gorillas by giving them milk from a baby bottle.

A safe home

Once a gorilla has lived with humans, it's very difficult to reintroduce it back to the wild. So we took the baby to a local sanctuary, a safe place where wild animals can be protected. He settled in really well, and was gradually introduced to an existing group of gorillas living at the sanctuary.

It's such a shame that this baby could not have grown up in the wild. But it was great to see him happily interacting with other gorillas at the sanctuary – and to know he was saved from an unpleasant fate.

The gorillas in their wildlife sanctuary are pretty safe, as they are protected by fences.

CAN WE SAVE THE GORILLA?

Will gorillas survive - or could they die out and become extinct? Conservation groups around the world are working incredibly hard to try to save gorillas, but it's a tough battle to win.

These amazing creatures will continue to be in danger unless we can solve their problems soon.

Serious trouble

It might seem strange that gorillas are so endangered, as there are still up to 200,000 of them in the wild. That's much more than some other endangered species, such as the tiger or the giant panda.

But gorillas face a deadly mixture of problems. Habitat loss and poaching are bad enough – but the killer disease Ebola makes things even worse. Some experts think that if Ebola spreads through Africa's forests, gorillas could be all gone in 20 years.

Science solutions

On the plus side, Ebola is a problem that could be solved, if scientists can find a way to stop it in its tracks, or stop gorillas from catching it. As Ebola also affects humans, lots of scientists are hard at work on it.

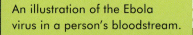

An illustration of the Ebola virus in a person's bloodstream.

Save the whole habitat

If we can save gorillas, they'll need somewhere to live – and the best place for gorillas to live is in the natural forests where they belong. The forest isn't just a home for the gorilla – it is an ecosystem, a living system made up of the land, the trees and all the other plants and animals that live there. Once an ecosystem is gone, it cannot be recreated – so we have to do everything we can to save it.

Visiting zoos is a great way to find out more about endangered species, and help them at the same time.

The tiger is another rare, endangered animal that you can see in the zoo, or adopt.

What can you do?

- **Visit the zoo** Have a day out and meet some real gorillas. Your entrance fee will help raise money, and you'll learn more about all sorts of amazing animals.
- **Adopt a gorilla** Lots of zoos and wildlife charities have adopt-an-animal schemes. You pay some money to help look after a gorilla, and receive updates on its progress.

- **Be an ecotourist** You might be able to visit a national park on holiday, to go wildlife-watching.
- **Work in conservation!** If you're really keen, maybe you could become a zookeeper, wildlife vet, conservation worker or scientist. Start by choosing science subjects at school, especially biology.

ABOUT ZSL

The Zoological Society of London (ZSL) is a charity that provides conservation support for animals both in the UK and worldwide. We also run ZSL London Zoo and ZSL Whipsnade Zoo.

Our work in the wild extends to Africa, where our conservationists and scientists are working to protect gorillas from extinction. These astounding apes are part of ZSL's EDGE of Existence programme, which is specially designed to focus on genetically distinct animals that are struggling for survival.

By buying this book, you have helped us raise money to continue our conservation work with gorillas and other animals in need of protection. Thank you.

To find out more about ZSL and how you can become further involved with our work visit **zsl.org** and **zsl.org/edge**

The world's gorillas need their wild forest homes to survive.

ZSL
LIVING CONSERVATION

EDGE

ZSL
LONDON
ZOO

ZSL
WHIPSNADE
ZOO

Websites

Western gorilla at EDGE of Existence
www.zsl.org/edgegorilla

Gorilla Kingdom at ZSL London Zoo
www.zsl.org/gorillakingdom

Adopt a gorilla at ZSL London Zoo
www.zsl.org/adoptgorilla

Gorilla Conservation at ZSL
www.zsl.org/gorillaconservation

Places to visit

ZSL London Zoo
Outer Circle, Regent's Park, London,
NW1 4RY, UK
www.zsl.org/london
0844 225 1826

The gorilla group at ZSL London Zoo is helping to inspire future conservationists.

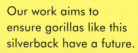

Our work aims to ensure gorillas like this silverback have a future.

GLOSSARY

breed Mate and have babies.

browse Leafy branches used as food for animals.

bushmeat Meat that comes from wild animals.

Conservation breeding Breeding animals in captivity.

captivity Being kept in a zoo, wildlife park or garden.

civil war A war between different sides within the same country.

climate The normal weather patterns in a particular place.

conservation Protecting nature and wildlife.

conservation status How endangered a living thing is.

critically endangered Very seriously endangered and at risk of extinction

ecosystem A habitat and the living things that are found in it.

ecotourism Visiting wild places as a tourist to see wildlife.

EDGE Short for Evolutionarily Distinct and Globally Endangered.

enclosure A secure pen, cage or other home or for a zoo animal.

endangered At risk of dying out and become extinct.

extinct No longer existing.

forage To search around for food.

habitat The natural surroundings that a species lives in.

habitat loss Damaging or destroying habitat.

IUCN Short for the International Union for Conservation of Nature

logging Cutting down trees.

mammal A kind of animal that feeds its babies on milk from its body.

monitor To check, measure or keep track of something.

national park A protected area of land where wildlife can live safely.

park ranger Someone who patrols and guards a national park.

poaching Hunting animals that are protected by law and shouldn't be hunted.

population Number of people, or animals, in a particular place.

primates Group of animals that includes humans, apes and monkeys.

range The area where an animal or species lives.

re-introduce To release a species back into the wild.

shoot The first growth of a plant from a seed.

silverback An older male gorilla with silver hair on his back.

species A particular type of living thing.

studbook A record of the animals of a particular species born in captivity.

subspecies Different types of an animal within one main species.

Swahili A language spoken in eastern Africa.

tracking Finding or following wild animals by their signs and marks.

troop A family group of gorillas.

ultrasound scan A way of using sound waves to look inside the body.

vaccine Medicine to stop you from getting a particular disease.

vitamins Chemicals that your body needs, found ion some foods.

vulnerable At risk, but not as seriously as an endangered species.

wildlife reserve A protected area of land where wildlife can live safely.

ZSL Short for Zoological Society of London.

FIND OUT MORE

Books

What's it Like to be a... Zoo Keeper? by Elizabeth Dowen and Lisa Thompson, A&C Black 2010

Gorillas: Life in the Troop by Willow Clark, Powerkids Press 2011

Amazing Animals: Gorillas by Stephan Brewer, Gareth Stevens Publishing 2010

My Top 20 Endangered Animals by Steve Parker, Miles Kelly Publishing, 2010

Websites

Western lowland gorillas at Brookfield Zoo
www.brookfieldzoo.org/czs/Brookfield/Exhibit-and-Animal-Guide/Tropic-World/Western-Lowland-Gorilla

Gorilla webcams at Bristol Zoo
www.bristolzoo.org.uk/webcams

Places to visit

Bristol Zoo Gardens
Clifton, Bristol, BS8 3HA, UK
www.bristolzoo.org.uk/
0117 974 7399

**Durrell Wildlife Park
(also known as Jersey Zoo)**
La Profonde Rue, Trinity, Jersey,
Channel Islands JE3 5BP
www.durrell.org/Wildlife-park

Belfast Zoo
Antrim Road, Belfast BT36 7PN,
Northern Ireland, UK
www.belfastzoo.co.uk

San Francisco Zoo
Sloat Blvd. & Great Highway,
San Francisco, CA 94132, USA
www.sfzoo.org

Brookfield Zoo
8400 31st Street, Brookfield,
IL 60513, Chicago, USA
www.brookfieldzoo.org

INDEX

OTHER TITLES IN THE ANIMALS ON THE EDGE SERIES

www.storiesfromthezoo.com

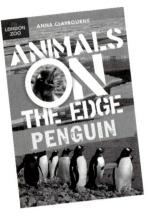

Penguin
ISBN: HB 978-1-4081-4822-8
PB 978-1-4081-4960-7

Rhino
ISBN: HB 978-1-4081-4823-5
PB 978-1-4081-4956-0

Tiger
ISBN: HB 978-1-4081-4824-2
PB 978-1-4081-4957-7

Hippo
ISBN: HB 978-1-4081-4826-6
PB 978-1-4081-4961-4

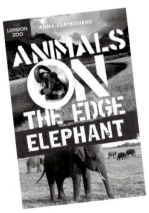

Elephant
ISBN: HB 978-1-4081-4827-3
PB 978-1-4081-4958-4